For Roddy, Lawson
and Noah – **A.S.**

For Isaac – **J.S.**

Amy Sparkes is donating 5% of her royalties to Tommy's (registered charity number 1060508).
Tommy's exists to save babies' lives through funding research and providing information.
To find out more visit www.tommys.org

First published in 2015 by Scholastic Children's Books
Euston House, 24 Eversholt Street
London NW1 1DB
a division of Scholastic Ltd
www.scholastic.co.uk
London · New York · Toronto · Sydney · Auckland
Mexico City · New Delhi · Hong Kong

Text copyright © 2015 Amy Sparkes
Illustrations copyright © 2015 Jamie Smith

PB ISBN 978 1407 16147 1

ALIEN'S CRAZY CHRISTMAS

Amy Sparkes ✦ **Jamie Smith**

SCHOLASTIC

An alien came down to Earth one snowy **Christmas Day**.

It looked so **fun** and **jolly** he was sad to come away.

Zobble said, "We need a **Christmas** back on **Planet Blip!**"

Carefully he wrote his notes and made a shopping trip.

But as he **whizzed off** through the sky, the spaceship **span** around—

It **scattered** Zobble's notes about and turned them **upside down**.

"What a **mess!**" cried Zobble as he rearranged the lot.

"I hope I can remember now which goes with who and what!"

At last he sighed with great relief, "I *think* I've worked it out.

But what on Earth do Earthlings do

with all these **Brussels sprouts?**"

On **Planet Blip,** the *Stop Here Santa*
sign went in the ground.
Then Zobble called to all his friends,
"Come on now, gather round!

We're going to have a **Christmas** -
it will cheer you up – you'll see!
Now first of all we decorate
this lovely **Christmas Tree!"**

The tree was looking beautiful
when Zobble cried, "OH, STOP!
I think the Christmas turkey's got to go up **on the top!**"

But **Turkey** didn't want to be
at such a dizzy height,
So when they went to grab him,
Turkey **ran** with all his might.

BRUSSELS SPROUTS

Zobble sighed, "Well, never mind! Try something else instead –
Our **underwear** should hang there, at the end of **every** bed.
But what should be **inside** them? I know what would be jolly –
Let's fill the socks and pants up with some **mistletoe** and **holly!**"

"Christmas isn't very fun," the aliens all said.

"Perhaps we should **forget it**

and do something else instead."

"Oh, don't give up," begged Zobble. "Now **this** will hit the spot!

Just wait until we shove the **reindeer** down the chimney pot!"

They **heaved** and **huffed** and **pushed** and **puffed** –

he wouldn't move a hoof.

There was **NO WAY**, without a sleigh, he was getting on that roof!

Zobble sighed and read his notes, "We *must* throw **balls of snow**.
These **little pies** will do instead – let's give this snow a go!"

The aliens were **puzzled**, "Are you *sure* you've got this right?"

As pastry started flying in a messy mince-pie fight.

Just then a sleigh came down to land and **Santa Claus** appeared.

"That *Stop Here Santa* sign is new," he said and stroked his beard.

But then his eyes popped open wide, he dropped his heavy sack.

"**My missing reindeer!**" Santa cried and ran to get him back.

"**Santa, wait!**" groaned Zobble – oh, everything was **wrong!**

"Oh dear, let's try a Christmas play and sing a Christmas song."

They squeezed the **donkey** in the crib, and brought him gifts galore,

But when they stepped in Donkey's poo – it was **the final straw!**

"We've **had enough** of Christmas!" the aliens all wailed.

"We're more fed-up than **ever**! Your Christmas plan has **failed!**"

Just then the turkey **hurtled** through, it didn't see the danger –

And with a **C** **R**

Stop Here Santa

A S H!

it **knocked** the donkey right out of the manger.

The donkey landed right on Santa,
with a noisy **THUMP!**

They backed into the Christmas tree
with an almighty **BUMP!**

It wibble-wobbled,

Poor Zobble **slipped**

and then he **tripped,**

and fell flat on his tummy.

A **sprout** shot right into his mouth. He cried,
"It's yummy-scrummy!"

He licked his lips, and grinned with joy,
"At last I've worked it out!
That's what on Earth you're meant to do –
EAT the Brussels sprout!"

Zobble dashed to make a **feast** then called for everyone.

"There's one last chance to show them all that Christmas **can** be fun."

Nervous as they gathered round, he clenched his spiky teeth

He lifted up the tablecloth . . . and **what** was underneath . . . ?

"**What a feast!**" the aliens said. "The like we've never seen!
And best of all it's absolutely gooey, gloopy **green!**"

"But you didn't **stuff** the turkey," Santa said and scratched his head.
Zobble gasped, "Oh, **I forgot!** I'll do it now, instead."

So...

He ran around and served the bird until he **huffed** and **puffed**.

He made sure that the turkey was well and truly **stuffed!**

The aliens were **happy** now.

"At last we have **no** doubts.

Oh, we **love** Christmas!" they all cheered.
"Hurray for Brussels sprouts!"

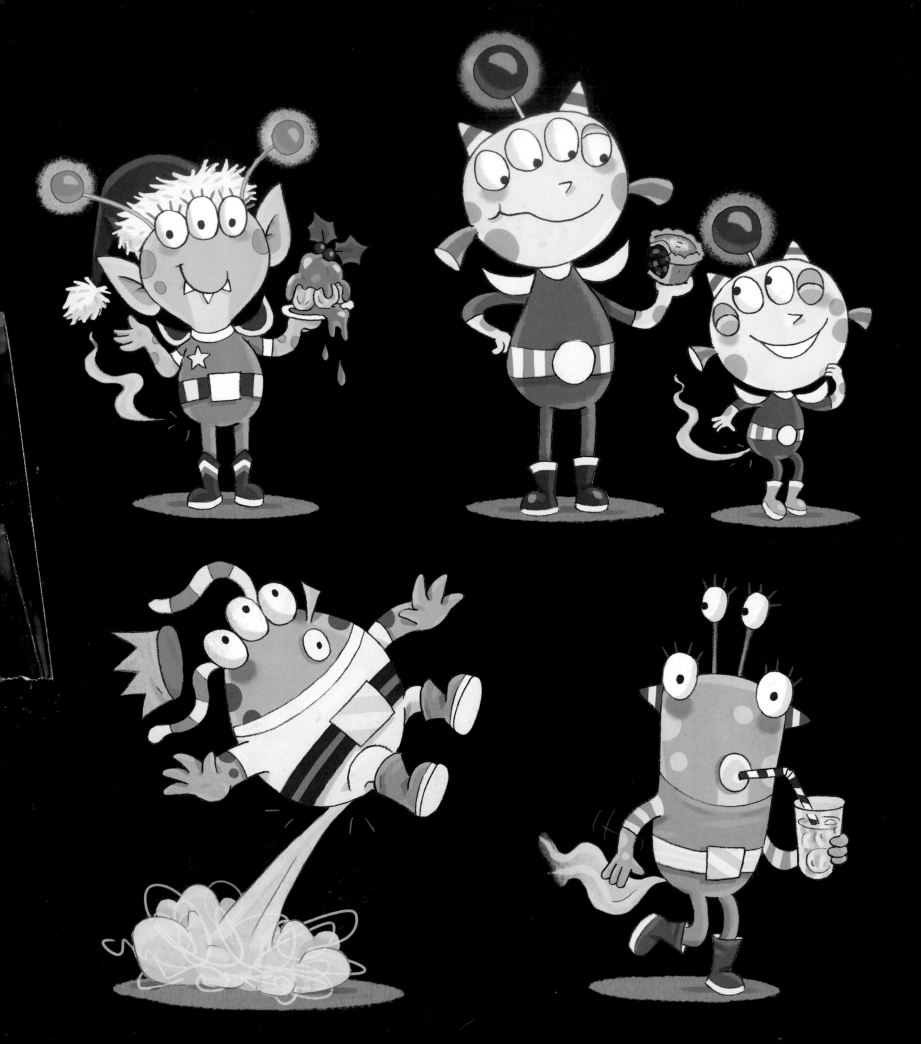

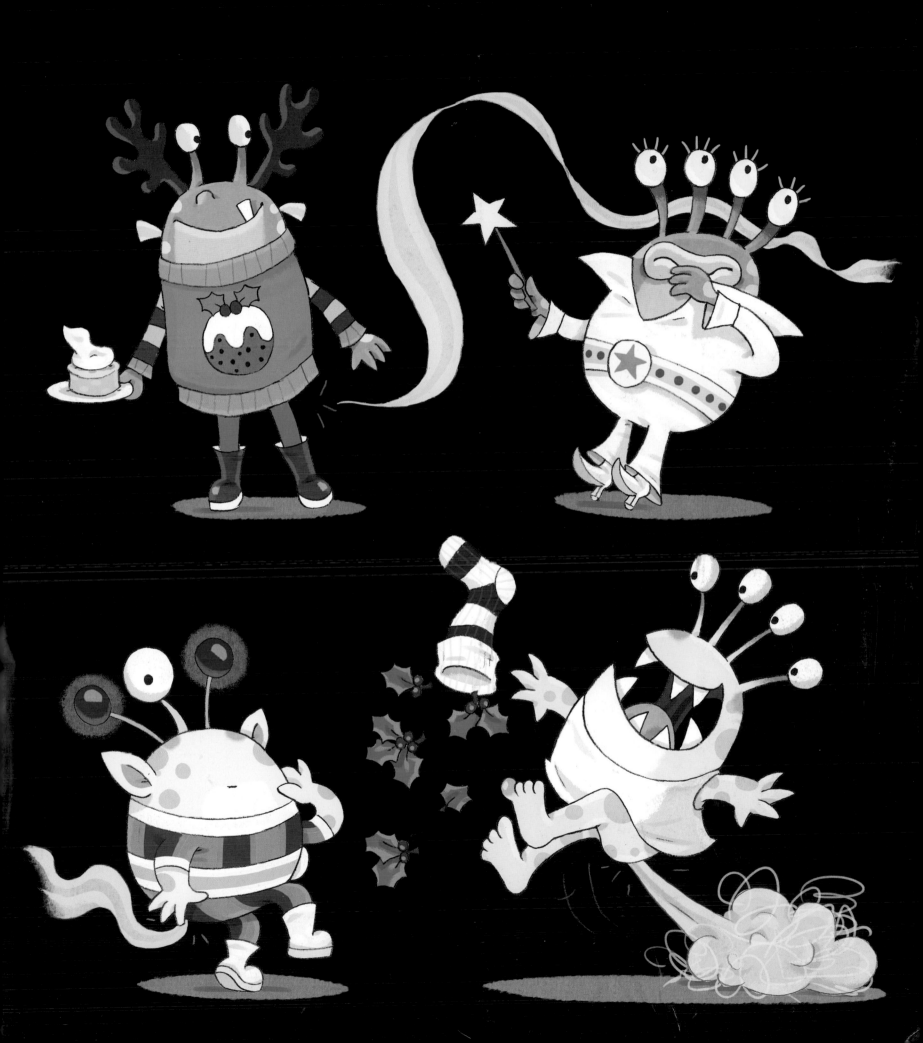